Steck-Vaughn

BRIDGES
TO
READING COMPREHENSION

Level B/C

STECK-VAUGHN
C O M P A N Y
ELEMENTARY · SECONDARY · ADULT · LIBRARY

ACKNOWLEDGMENTS

EXECUTIVE EDITOR: Diane Sharpe

PROJECT EDITOR: Anne Souby

DESIGN MANAGER: Donna Brawley

ELECTRONIC PRODUCTION (COVER): Alan Klemp

PHOTO EDITOR: Margie Foster

PRODUCT DEVELOPMENT: Curriculum Concepts

ILLUSTRATION CREDITS: Cover Adolph Gonzalez; Unit 1 Phil Scheuer: p.21; Kathleen Howell: p.34-36; Unit 2 Chet Jezierski: pp.45-51, 53-61, 63; Jan Naimo Jones: 64-71, 73-80, 82-83; Unit 3 Meryl Henderson: 86-95, 97-102, 105; Lyle Miller: 107-113, 116-123, 125.

PHOTO CREDITS: Unit 1 p.4 (food drive) © Myrleen Ferguson/PhotoEdit, (litter) © David Young-Wolff/PhotoEdit; p.6 © Eunice Harris/Photo Researchers; p.7 Courtesy Utah Tourist Bureau; pp.8-12 © The Ute Bulletin; p.13 Courtesy Utah Tourist Bureau; p.14 © Eunice Harris/Photo Researchers; p.15 © Michael Newman/PhotoEdit; p.16 © Myrleen Ferguson/PhotoEdit; p.17 © Lori Adamski/Tony Stone Images; pp.18-20 © Myrleen Ferguson/PhotoEdit; p.22 © Lori Adamski/Tony Stone Images; p.23 © Michael Newman/PhotoEdit; p.24, 28 © Peter Glass/Monkmeyer Press Photo Service; pp.25-27, 29, 31-32 © Terry Clark/ New York Times Pictures; pp.33,38 Courtesy Cathy Harraghy; Unit 2 p.42 (Mandela) © Ken Osterbroek/Gamma Liaison, (Eleanor Roosevelt) © UPI/Bettmann Newsphotos; p.44 © Anthony Blake/Tony Stone Images; Unit 3 p.84 David Young-Wolff/PhotoEdit; p.106 © F. Stuart Westmorland/Photo Researchers.

Grateful acknowledgment is made for permission
to reprint copyrighted material as follows:

New Friends in a New Land: A Thanksgiving Story by Judith Bauer Stamper.
Copyright © 1993 by Dialogue Systems, Inc.

The Hole in the Dike retold by Norma Green.
Copyright © 1974 by Norma B. Green.
Reprinted by permission of Scholastic, Inc.

George Washington Carver: Plant Doctor by Mirna Benitez.
Copyright © 1989 by American Teacher Publications.

The Last Snow of Winter by Tony Johnston.
Copyright © 1993 by Tony Johnston.
Reprinted by permission of Tambourine Books,
a division of William Morrow & Company, Inc.

ISBN 0–8114–5743–5

5 6 7 8 9 0   BP   00 99 98 97

CONTENTS

SUPER KIDS

What are super kids?

No, super kids can't leap over buildings! They aren't super strong. These kids are just like you. What makes them super? They all did something special they can be proud of.

Some of the things these kids did were hard. Some were scary. Some took hours of hard work. In this unit, you will read about kids who learn what it means to be super.

What Do You Already Know?

Think about the street where you live, your school, and your town. Are there some things you'd like to change? What could you do to make yourself feel proud? Write a paragraph about something special you'd like to do.

_____

_____

_____

_____

_____

_____

_____

What Do You Want to Find Out?

You will read about many kids who do things they are proud of. On the lines below, write some questions you would like to ask them. You may find the answers as you read.

_____

_____

_____

_____

_____

_____

_____

GETTING READY TO READ

The first story is called "A Statue for Grandpa." Can you imagine what it would be like to walk through a building and see a statue of someone in your family? Surprise—you didn't even know it was there!

What Do You Think You Will Learn?

Look through "A Statue for Grandpa" on pages 7–9. What do you think you will learn as you read this story? Write your ideas below.

_____

_____

_____

_____

_____

_____

A Statue
for Grandpa

Imagine seeing statues of your great grandfathers in your state capitol building. How proud you would feel! But what if those statues had no names on them? No one would know they were statues of your grandfathers. That's what happened to Rena and Jenna Duncan.

Rena and Jenna are Native American girls. They aren't sisters. They are aunt and niece, but they're the same age. They live in Utah. The girls like to ride horses, listen to music, and tell stories.

When Rena was about ten years old, she visited Salt Lake City. Salt Lake City is the capital of Utah. She went to the Utah State Capitol Building. There Rena saw two stone statues of Native Americans. She looked closely at the statues. One statue was of John Duncan, her great-great grandfather. The other statue was of Unca Som, her great-great-great grandfather! But no one else knew who these people were. The statues had no names on them.

This is the Utah State Capitol Building. The statues of Unca Som and John Duncan are in this building.

John Duncan was the last great chief of the Uintah Band of Ute Indians. Unca Som was an Indian medicine man who lived the old way of life.

Rena and Jenna wondered why the statues of their grandfathers had no name plates. A teacher named Dallas Murray also wondered why the statues were nameless. Mr. Murray grew up near the Ute Indian Reservation. He had seen the statues many times. He knew the statues were of John Duncan and Unca Som.

Mr. Murray found out about Jenna and Rena. He called the girls with an idea. He thought Rena and Jenna could help get name plates put on the statues.

These statues had no name plates on them. No one knew that they were John Duncan and Unca Som.

Rena is speaking to the lawmakers. Jenna is the young girl standing beside her.

Mr. Murray's idea was to ask the lawmakers to put name plates on the statues. Then the lawmakers would vote on this idea. Mr. Murray wanted the girls to speak to the lawmakers. Rena and Jenna would tell the lawmakers why they should vote yes.

The girls felt honored and proud. Jenna spoke to the lawmakers about Unca Som. She said Unca Som lived the old way of life. Today there are no true medicine men like Unca Som.

Then it was Rena's turn to speak to the lawmakers. Rena spoke about John Duncan. She told them that he was a great leader to his people. She said, "Even though I never knew him, he gives me pride to be an Indian."

The lawmakers voted. They voted yes. On January 16, 1990, Rena, Jenna, and Dallas Murray hung name plates on the statues. It was a happy day! Now John Duncan and Unca Som proudly watch over the Utah state lawmakers.

AFTER READING

What Did You Learn?

You have read "A Statue for Grandpa" for the first time. Now look back at what you wrote on page 6. Did you learn what you thought you would? What were you surprised to learn? Write two or three things you learned below.

_____

_____

_____

_____

_____

Check Your Understanding

Darken the circle next to the word or words that best complete each sentence.

1. Rena visited the Utah State Capitol Building in _____.

  Ⓐ Duncan   Ⓒ Salt Lake City

  Ⓑ Kansas City   Ⓓ Uintah

2. The statues Rena saw had no _____ plates on them.

  Ⓐ dinner   Ⓒ home

  Ⓑ horses   Ⓓ name

3. John Duncan was a _____ of the Uintah Band.

  Ⓐ chief   Ⓒ teacher

  Ⓑ medicine man   Ⓓ painter

4. Unca Som was a _____.

  Ⓐ teacher   Ⓒ medicine man

  Ⓑ painter   Ⓓ chief

Vocabulary — Context Clues

Sometimes you can figure out what a word means by looking at words around it. Read these sentences.

Rena and Jenna wondered why the statues of their grandfathers had no name plates. A teacher named Dallas Murray also wondered why the statues were nameless.

You can find the meaning of the word nameless from the words and sentences around it. From the words no name plates, you can tell that nameless means "no name."

Find the words below in "A Statue for Grandpa." Use the words around each word to figure out the meanings. Circle your answers.

1. statue (page 7)

    a. a stone figure or shape of someone

    b. a painting of someone

2. lawmakers (page 9)

    a. people who build statues

    b. people who make new laws

3. honored (page 9)

    a. proud

    b. felt bad

Words That Were New to You

Choose words from the story that were new to you. Use a dictionary to check the meanings. Add the words and their meanings to your word list on page 126.

REREADING

Main Idea and Details

A main idea tells what a paragraph is all about. It is the most important idea in a paragraph. Details give more information about the main idea. Sometimes you will read one sentence that gives the main idea. Sometimes you will have to come up with the main idea yourself. Read this paragraph.

Amy and Sue are best friends. They ride their horses after school. Amy rides Blackie. Sue rides Brownie. The two friends like to ride fast.

The first sentence tells the main idea. Amy and Sue are best friends. The other sentences tell the details. They tell about the girls' friendship.

As you reread "A Statue for Grandpa," write one detail to support each main idea below. Write your answers on the lines.

1. Main Idea: When Rena was about ten years old, she visited Salt Lake City. (page 7)

   DETAIL: _____

   _____

2. Main Idea: Mr. Murray's idea was to ask the lawmakers to put name plates on the statues. (page 9)

   DETAIL: _____

   _____

STUDY SKILLS

Alphabetical Order

Each letter of the alphabet has a special place or order. This is called **alphabetical order**. Alphabetical order helps you to find things quickly.

The words below are in alphabetical order. The word that begins with a comes first. The word that begins with b comes next. There are no words that begin with c. So the word that begins with d comes next.

American

building

Duncan

Jenna

Utah

Read these story words. Go through the alphabet and put the words in alphabetical order. Number them on the first lines as you go. Then, write the words on the next lines in alphabetical order.

1. _____ Utah   _____

   _____ Salt Lake City   _____

   _____ capital   _____

   _____ lawmakers   _____

2. _____ statues   _____

   _____ honored   _____

   _____ medicine   _____

   _____ chief   _____

Check Yourself

Pick four more words from the story. Go through the alphabet and put the words in alphabetical order.

THINK and WRITE

Use what you have learned to complete one of these activities.

1. Find out more about statues. How are they made? What are they made of? Use the encyclopedia or other books to help you. Write a short report.

2. Imagine you were Rena or Jenna. Write a short speech to give to the lawmakers. Tell why John Duncan and Unca Som should have their names on their statues.

3. If you could make a statue of someone in your family, who would you choose? Write a short paragraph telling why you would choose that person.

GETTING READY TO READ

This story is called "You're Super, Too!" What are the people in the picture doing? Why do you think they are doing it?

What Do You Think You Will Learn?

Look through "You're Super, Too!" on pages 16–18. What do you think you will learn as you read this story? Write your ideas below.

_____

_____

_____

_____

_____

_____

You're Super, Too

What can you do to make the world better? Lots! Getting started is the hardest part. First, choose something that is important to you. You might try to raise money to buy new T-shirts for a school team. You might work in the park on the weekends. Maybe you'd like to help out at an animal shelter or help homeless people.

Here are some ideas to help you get started.

Step 1   Become a Know-It-All

Learn everything you can about a problem. Read books, magazines, and newspapers.

Call and write to places that can give you help. If you pick recycling, write to the makers of cans or bottles.

Visit animal shelters and homes for older people. Ask the people who work there how you can help.

Become a Know-It-All!

These super kids are helping out at a shelter for homeless people.

Step 2   Roundup Time!

Get your friends to work with you. Problems get fixed faster when people work together. Teamwork is the key.

Find other people who are already working on the problem. Join them, or learn from them. What did they try? Did it work? Could that idea work for you?

Planting a tree is a job for this team of super kids!

Step 3   Ideas Are You!

Now think about how you can help fix the problem. Get the team together and brainstorm. Brainstorming is thinking up ideas. Write down all the ideas your team dreams up. Write down the good ideas. Write down the silly ideas, too. Sometimes, the wildest ideas are the ones that work best.

Step 4   Get the Word Out

Start with your school newspaper. Write about the problem. Tell about your ideas for fixing it. Think of a fun, catchy name for your group's plan. Catchy names might interest TV news shows.

TV and radio shows like stories about kids who try to make things better. Many people will hear about your work if news shows talk about it. More people might want to join your team. More people means more work can get done!

Making posters is a great way to get the word out.

Step 5   Now Get to Work!

Put your plan to work. Work hard at it. If your plan doesn't work, try another idea. Super kids don't give up. They know that with hard work they can change the world for the better!

AFTER READING

What Did You Learn?

You have read "You're Super, Too!" for the first time. Now look back at what you wrote on page 15. Did you learn what you thought you would learn? What was the most useful idea? Write two or three useful ideas below.

_____

_____

_____

Check Your Understanding

Darken the circle next to the word or words that best complete each sentence.

1. Kids can help _____ the world for the better.

   Ⓐ change   Ⓒ practice

   Ⓑ teach   Ⓓ turn

2. Try to _____ everything you can about a problem.

   Ⓐ buy   Ⓒ sell

   Ⓑ make   Ⓓ learn

3. People can work on problems faster when they work _____.

   Ⓐ one by one   Ⓒ alone

   Ⓑ together   Ⓓ quietly

4. One way to get the word out about your plan is your school _____.

   Ⓐ club   Ⓒ class

   Ⓑ newspaper   Ⓓ library

Vocabulary — Compound Words

Two smaller words are sometimes put together to make a new word. The new word is called a compound word. The smaller words can help you figure out the compound word. Sometimes they can help you with the meaning.

Read this sentence.

Start with your school newspaper.

Newspaper is made up of two smaller words, news and paper. Think about each of the smaller words. It will help you figure out that newspaper means "a paper that gives the news."

Underline the compound word in each sentence. Then write the two smaller words that make up the compound word on the lines.

1. One way to think up new ideas is to brainstorm with your friends.

   _____   _____

2. Schools recycle cans to raise money for the baseball team.

   _____   _____

3. Spend one day each weekend helping out.

   _____   _____

4. Teamwork will get the job done faster.

   _____   _____

Words That Were New to You

Choose words from the story that were new to you. Use a dictionary to check the meanings. Add the words and their meanings to your word list on page 126.

REREADING

Sequence

When you read a story that tells how to do something, think about the order of the steps. What do you do first? What is next? What do you do after that?

Look at the pictures.

You can tell by looking at the pictures what steps these kids took. First, they read about a recycling drive at school. Then, they collected cans. Next, they took them to the recycling center. Finally, they changed the sign.

Reread "You're Super, Too!" Then, put the steps in the right order. Write 1, 2, 3, 4, or 5 on the lines in front of each step.

_____ Get the word out about the project.

_____ Brainstorm for good ideas.

_____ Get to work.

_____ Round up all your friends.

_____ Learn what you can about the problem.

Main Idea and Details

Main ideas are the big, important ideas in a story.

1. Underline the sentence that tells the main idea in "You're Super, Too!"

   Collect cans and newspapers to recycle.

   Kids can help change the world.

   Write letters to town leaders.

Details are small parts of the big or main idea.

2. Underline all the details from the story.

   Teamwork will solve the problem faster.

   Kids like to be on TV.

   Think of a fun name for your project.

STUDY SKILLS

Follow Directions

Directions tell you how to do something. Be sure to read all of the steps in the directions before you start. Look for words that tell you what to do.

Read the directions below for ideas on how to brainstorm.

▶ Work in a small group.

▶ Pick a person to write down the ideas.

▶ Only one person should talk at a time.

▶ Everyone should listen while a person talks.

▶ No one should say things like "that's bad" or "what a stupid idea."

▶ Let everyone pick or vote for the best ideas.

Use the directions for how to brainstorm to answer the questions below. Write the answers on the lines.

1. What is the first thing you should do?

_____

2. What does one person write?

_____

3. What do you do while someone is talking?

_____

4. What do you do last?

_____

Check Yourself

Ask three friends to brainstorm with you. Think of some ideas to start a recycling drive at your school.

THINK and WRITE

Use the ideas in "You're Super, Too!" to complete one of these activities.

1. List four things you like to do. Next to each one, write one way you could use that activity to help others.

2. Brainstorm with your friends for ideas that would help your school. Write a list of your best ideas.

3. Find four places in your town where children could help out. Write a short paragraph about what children could do at each place.

GETTING READY TO READ

Have you ever dreamed about doing something really super? How could you make your dream come true? The next story you will read is called "The Young Pilot." It's about a girl with dreams. What do you think the girl in the story wants to do?

What Do You Think You Will Learn?

Look through "The Young Pilot" on pages 25–27. What do you think you will learn as you read this story? Write your ideas below.

_____

_____

_____

_____

_____

_____

THE YOUNG PILOT

Meet Vicki Van Meter. She's a lot like other kids. She goes to school. She likes stuffed animals and baseball cards. And she dreams of someday being an astronaut. But there is something that makes Vicki different from other kids. She is the youngest girl to fly an airplane across the United States. She is also the youngest girl to fly all the way across the Atlantic Ocean.

Vicki made her flight across the United States when she was only 11. Vicki lives in Pennsylvania, but her flight started in Maine. She flew all the way from Maine to California. That is 2,900 miles!

You might think that it took Vicki many years to become a pilot. But it didn't. Vicki started flying about a year before her trip across the United States.

This is Vicki Van Meter. One day she hopes to become an astronaut.

This is the plane that Vicki flew across the United States.

It all started in 1992 when Vicki was only 10 years old. One day she and her father saw an ad for a flight school. A flight school is a place where people learn to fly airplanes.

Vicki's dad knew that Vicki dreamed of someday being an astronaut. Flying a plane would be a great place to start! He asked her if she wanted to sign up for a flying lesson. Vicki jumped at the chance.

Vicki loved the feeling of being high off the ground. Soon Vicki and her flight teacher were flying all the time. She started going on longer and longer trips. And then she dreamed up a super plan. She wanted to fly all the way across the country.

The law says that a pilot under 16 must fly with an older pilot. When it was time for Vicki to fly across the country, her teacher was at her side. But Vicki was the one doing the flying.

Vicki made it all the way cross country! Many people wanted to talk with her. People wrote newspaper stories about her. She got to be on TV talk shows. She even met Vice President Al Gore! He showed Vicki and all her class around the White House.

Vicki was proud of herself. But now she had another dream. She wanted to fly across the Atlantic Ocean!

Flying across the ocean would be much harder. Most of the time she would be flying over water. She would not be able to make any stops at all. Vicki learned how to get out of the plane if there was trouble.

In June 1994, Vicki and her teacher made the trip. Vicki became the youngest girl ever to fly a plane across the Atlantic Ocean. Now she will be remembered as a super pilot along with Charles Lindbergh and Amelia Earhart. Charles Lindbergh was the first man to fly across the Atlantic Ocean. He made his trip in 1927. Amelia Earhart was the first woman to fly across the Atlantic Ocean. Her trip was in 1932.

Now Vicki has a new dream. When she becomes an astronaut, she wants to take a trip to Mars! And Vicki has already shown that dreams can come true!

Vicki likes to collect baseball cards.

AFTER READING

What Did You Learn?

You have read "The Young Pilot" for the first time. Now look back at what you wrote on page 24. Did you learn what you thought you would learn? What surprised you about Vicki Van Meter? Write two things you learned about her below.

_____

_____

_____

Check Your Understanding

Darken the circle next to the word that best completes each sentence.

1. Vicki lives in _____.

   Ⓐ Maine   Ⓒ Pennsylvania

   Ⓑ California   Ⓓ TV

2. Vicki learned to _____ at flight school.

   Ⓐ teach   Ⓒ dream

   Ⓑ fly   Ⓓ jump

3. Vicki wants to become an _____.

   Ⓐ teacher   Ⓒ pilot

   Ⓑ astronaut   Ⓓ lawyer

4. Vicki visited the White House with her _____.

   Ⓐ TV   Ⓒ airplane

   Ⓑ newspaper   Ⓓ class

Vocabulary — Synonyms and Antonyms

Sometimes one word in a sentence helps you figure out the meaning of another word. Read these sentences.

> Vicki did not **start** to fly until she was 10. That's when she decided to **begin** taking lessons.

The words in dark print are synonyms. Start and begin have the same meaning.

Words with opposite meanings are antonyms. They can also give clues to new words. Look at this sentence.

> The law says that a pilot **under** 16 years old must fly with a pilot **over** 16 years old.

Under and over are antonyms. The opposite of under is over.

Read the sentences below. Find the words in dark print. If the words are synonyms, write an S on the line. If they are antonyms, write an A.

_____ **1.** Vicki started flying on **short** trips. After a while she went on **long** trips.

_____ **2.** Vicki was **happy** about taking flight lessons. She was **glad** to go to the school.

_____ **3.** Vicki's trip **began** in Maine. It **ended** in California.

_____ **4.** Amelia Earhart was the **first** woman to fly across the Atlantic Ocean. Vicki probably won't be the **last.**

Words That Were New to You

Choose words from the story that were new to you. Use a dictionary to check the meanings. Add the words and their meanings to your word list on page 126.

REREADING

Compare and Contrast

When you compare two or more things, you tell how they are alike. When you contrast two or more things, you tell how they are different.

A chart can help you show how things are alike and how they are different. Look at this chart. It is about Vicki's trip across the United States and her trip across the ocean.

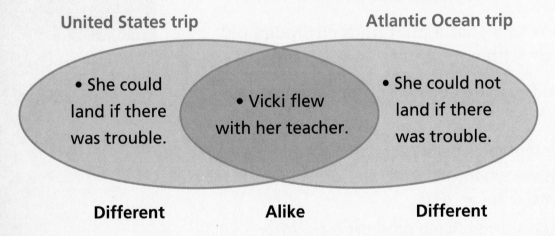

United States trip

Atlantic Ocean trip

- She could land if there was trouble.
- Vicki flew with her teacher.
- She could not land if there was trouble.

Different   **Alike**   **Different**

The chart helps you to see the difference between Vicki's two trips.

Reread "The Young Pilot." Then finish the chart. Use the story to help you.

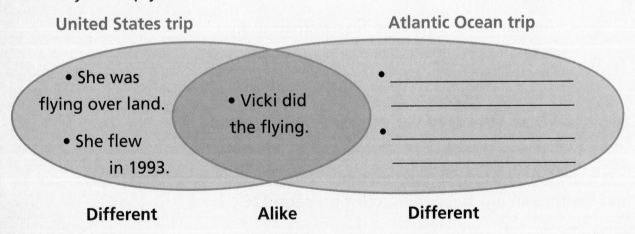

United States trip

Atlantic Ocean trip

- She was flying over land.
- She flew in 1993.
- Vicki did the flying.
- _____
- _____
- _____
- _____

Different   **Alike**   **Different**

Sequence

When you read, think about the order that things happen. Ask yourself what happened first? What happened next? What happened last?

Put these sentences in order. Write 1, 2, 3, or 4 in front of each sentence. Look at the story for help.

_____ Vicki flew across the Atlantic Ocean.

_____ Vicki flew across the United States.

_____ Vicki learned to fly.

_____ Vicki was invited to TV talk shows.

STUDY SKILLS

Dictionary — Guide Words

Words in the dictionary are listed in alphabetical order. The dictionary also has guide words to help you.

Suppose you want to look up the meaning of the word pilot. Guide words can help you find it. Look at part of a dictionary page below.

The words pen and place are guide words. They tell you that the first word on the page is pen and the last word on the page is place.

Here's how to find out if pilot is on this page.

P ▶ Look at the first letter. (**p**en **p**lace)

   P is in both guide words.

I ▶ Look at the second letter. (pen place)

   I comes between E and L. (e f g h i j k l)

   Pilot will be on this page.

> pen / place
> _____
> **pen** [pen] *noun* 1. a
> small yard for animals.
> 2. instrument used
> for writing.

Read the words in the box. For each word find the guide words below that would be on the same page as the word. Write the word on the line.

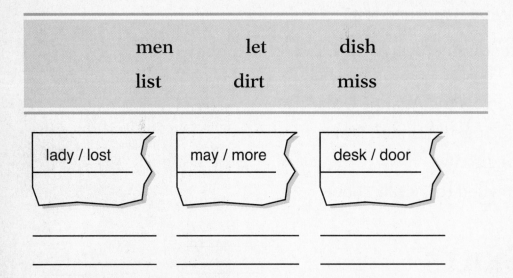

men	let	dish
list	dirt	miss

lady / lost _____

may / more _____

desk / door _____

_____   _____   _____

_____   _____   _____

Check Yourself

Look up a new word in the dictionary. What guide words are on the page?

THINK and WRITE

Use what you have learned to complete one of these activities.

1. Imagine you are a newspaper reporter. Write a short news story about Vicki Van Meter. Make a map to go with the story that shows how far she went.

2. Imagine you are Vicki. What would you tell your friends about your flights? Write what you would say about being a pilot.

3. Have you ever been on a plane trip? What was it like? Find out more about airplanes in an encyclopedia. Write about what you find out.

GETTING READY TO READ

Imagine moving a mountain of garbage. In this story, "They Bumped the Dump," some kids at Bridge Academy in Springfield, Massachusetts, move garbage. How do you think they will do it?

What Do You Think You Will Learn?

Look through "They Bumped the Dump" on pages 34–36. What do you think you will learn as you read this story? Write your ideas below.

_____

_____

_____

_____

_____

_____

They Bumped the Dump

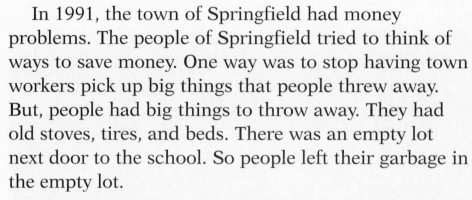

In 1991, the town of Springfield had money problems. The people of Springfield tried to think of ways to save money. One way was to stop having town workers pick up big things that people threw away. But, people had big things to throw away. They had old stoves, tires, and beds. There was an empty lot next door to the school. So people left their garbage in the empty lot.

Whenever Ms. Harraghy looked out her classroom window, she saw garbage. Students who went to school there didn't like the dump next door. "Who wants to go to school next to a dump?" Lisa said. "It makes us feel like we are dirty."

Miguel was in Lisa's class. He said, "The dump is a real big pile. There is no fence. Kids could get hurt."

The principal called City Hall about the dump. Nothing happened. Ms. Harraghy's class made a plan. The class called the plan Bump the Dump.

First, the class wrote a letter to the people in charge of the city. The letter said the dump was unhealthy and unsafe. There was no fence to keep kids out. Kids could cut themselves on things with sharp edges. The letter said the garbage should be removed.

The class also made posters. The posters were put up around the school. Some students called city leaders. Another student called the newspaper. Everyone worked together.

Then, things started to happen. A writer from the newspaper came. She wrote a story about the dump for the newspaper. Other people came to the school to talk about the dump.

Finally, the city leaders listened to Ms. Harraghy's class. They held a special meeting to talk about the dump.

Zulma was going to speak for the class. She had never made a speech before. Zulma told the city leaders why the dump was unsafe. She told them why the dump was unhealthy.

She also told them that the school did not have a gym. Zulma said the lot would make a good playground. The playground would be good for the school. It would be good for everyone who lived near the school, too.

The city sent workers to remove the garbage. "When I saw them cleaning up the dump I felt very proud," Lisa said. It took them a full week to clean the dump. The garbage filled eight trucks.

Ms. Harraghy's class did more than get the dump bumped. They learned how a city works. They learned about teamwork. They learned how good it feels to be part of a group that gets things done.

Zulma said, "The part I enjoyed most was seeing the class united. We became friends. It gave us a chance to learn from each other."

Lisa agreed. "I was very shy. I wouldn't speak to anyone. It was the best thing I ever did."

There is still no playground on the lot. Springfield still has money problems. But who knows. One day other kids might get together and figure out a way to get that playground. Kid power is super power!

AFTER READING

What Did You Learn?

You have read "They Bumped the Dump" for the first time. Now look back at what you wrote on page 33. Did you learn what you thought you would learn? What were you surprised to learn? Write two or three interesting things you learned.

_____

_____

_____

Check Your Understanding

Darken the circle next to the word or words that best complete each sentence.

1. A _____ was next door to the school.

  Ⓐ parking lot   Ⓒ mall

  Ⓑ school   Ⓓ dump

2. The students worked to get the _____ removed.

  Ⓐ cars   Ⓒ playground

  Ⓑ garbage   Ⓓ garden

3. They wrote letters and spoke to _____.

  Ⓐ city leaders   Ⓒ the police

  Ⓑ teachers   Ⓓ the principal

4. A story about "Bump the Dump" was in the _____.

  Ⓐ mountain   Ⓒ newspaper

  Ⓑ neighborhood   Ⓓ school

Vocabulary — Prefixes un- and re-

A prefix is a word part that is added to the beginning of a word. When you add a prefix to a word, it changes the meaning of the word. Look at these prefixes and their meanings. Then, read the sentences.

Prefix	Meaning
un-	not
re-	again

The dump was unsafe.

The kids wanted to rebuild it.

In the first sentence, the prefix un- is added to the word safe. So, unsafe means "not safe." In the second sentence, the prefix re- is added to the word build. So, rebuild means "to build again."

Read these sentences. Circle the words with prefixes. Write the meanings of the words with prefixes on the lines.

1. The kids were unhappy because the dump was a mess.

_____

2. It is unhealthy to leave out piles of garbage.

_____

3. The kids wrote and rewrote letters.

_____

Words That Were New to You

Choose words from the story that were new to you. Use a dictionary to check the meanings. Add the words and their meanings to your word list on page 126.

REREADING

Word Referents

A **pronoun** is a word that can stand for a noun. A **noun** names a person, place, or thing. Look at these pronouns.

I	me	you	he
she	it	we	they

Read these sentences.

> Zulma was going to speak for the class. She said the dump was unsafe.

The pronoun she stands for the noun Zulma.

Read the sentences below. Circle the noun that goes with each pronoun in dark print.

1. People had things to throw away. **They** left their garbage in the lot.

2. Miguel was in Lisa's class. **He** said, "Kids could get hurt."

3. The students decided to clean up the lot. **They** called their plan Bump the Dump.

4. Zulma was going to speak for the class. **She** went to the special meeting.

Reread "They Bumped the Dump." Look for pronouns. Find the noun that each pronoun stands for. Then, look on page 34. Find one place where a pronoun stands for a noun. Write the sentence or sentences with the noun and the pronoun on the lines. Underline the pronoun. Circle the noun.

Compare and Contrast

Complete the compare and contrast chart. Look back at the story to help you.

	Before the lot became a dump	After the lot became a dump
What happened to big things people threw away?	city workers took them away	
What was the lot next to the school like?	empty	
Did the school have a playground?	no	

STUDY SKILLS

Graphs

This **bar graph** shows how much money was raised each week for a new playground. It tells about five weeks.

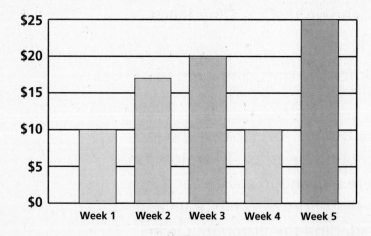

Look at the first bar on the graph. The top of the bar stops on the line next to $10. It shows how much was raised in week 1. Look at the second bar. It stops between $15 and $20. So, about $17 or $18 was raised in week 2.

Use the bar graph to answer the questions. Write the answers on the lines below.

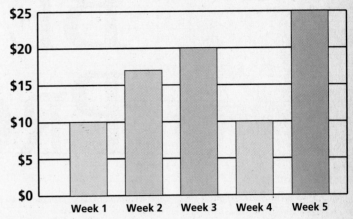

1. In which week was the most money

raised? _____

2. In which weeks was the same amount of money raised?

_____

3. In which weeks was the smallest

amount of money raised? _____

Check Yourself

Find a bar graph in your math book. What information does it give?

Use what you have learned to complete one of these activities.

1. Write a short story about something that needs fixing. Pick something in your school or where you live.

2. Suppose you could speak to city leaders about something that needs fixing in your town. What would you say? Write a short speech.

3. The kids made Bump the Dump posters. Make your own poster to tell about the plan. Tell why the dump should be moved.

2 BE PROUD

What makes people proud?

Did you ever feel really good about something a friend or someone in your family did? You were proud of that person!

People are proud of many things. Most people are proud of those who have done things for their country. In this unit, you will read two stories about people in two different countries. Each did something to be proud about!

What Do You Already Know?

Are you proud of one of your friends or someone in your family? What special things has the person done? Write a paragraph about someone who makes you proud. Tell how you feel about that person.

_____

_____

_____

_____

_____

_____

_____

What Do You Want to Find Out?

You will find out about people who did something special. What would you like to learn about these people? On the lines below, write some questions you want answered. You may find the answers to your questions as you read.

_____

_____

_____

_____

_____

_____

_____

GETTING READY TO READ

"New Friends in a New Land" is the first story in this unit. It is about people in America long ago. It tells about a Thanksgiving feast among new friends. Some of the people are made up, but some were really there at the first Thanksgiving. What do you do for Thanksgiving at your house?

What Do You Think You Will Learn?

Look through Part 1 of "New Friends in a New Land" on pages 45–48. Look at the people in the pictures. Think about the story name. Who do you think the new friends are? What do you think you will learn about them? Write your ideas below.

_____

_____

_____

_____

_____

New Friends in a New Land

PART 1

Damaris Hopkins sat on her father's knee in front of the kitchen fire. Beside her, Mrs. Hopkins held baby Oceanus. Her brother Giles and sister Constance sat nearby.

It was the year 1621. Just a few months ago, Damaris had come to America from England. She and her family had sailed on the ship called the *Mayflower*. Now they lived in a village called Plymouth.

Damaris looked into the fire and wished for the hundredth time that winter was over. She knew that food was running short. People were dying of sickness. And everyone worried about the Indians. The Indians lived on the land around Plymouth first. What would happen if they wanted their land back?

Damaris shivered and drew closer to her father. Her father hugged her and her mother gave her a smile. Damaris smiled bravely back.

A few days later, Damaris woke up early and pushed open the front door. The sun was just coming up over the rooftops.

Damaris sniffed the air. Something was different about it. It smelled like spring!

Damaris ran inside and shouted that spring was here. Oceanus started to cry, but the rest of the family laughed.

After her morning chores, Damaris ran outside to watch Father and Giles. They were adding thatch to the roof.

Just then, Damaris looked down the street. She could hardly believe her eyes!

A tall Indian was walking into Plymouth.

"Welcome, Englishmen," he said.

Damaris hid behind a fence and watched him. He carried a bow and two arrows. His black hair hung long in back.

The Indian called himself Samoset. He had learned some English from explorers. He was eager to talk to the Pilgrims. And they had many questions to ask him. The Pilgrims were glad that Samoset could talk to them in English.

Samoset told them about the land where Plymouth was built. The Patuxet (PUH tuks et) Indians had cleared it. But they had all died of a great sickness. After that no other Indians wanted the land.

The Pilgrims were glad to have Samoset as a friend. They gave him cheese, biscuits, and duck to eat. And they gave him a coat to wear.

Damaris watched Samoset all day. He seemed friendly. But Damaris knew almost nothing about Indians. She felt a little afraid but curious at the same time.

The sun began to set in the sky. Mrs. Hopkins came running in to tell the children the news. She said Samoset was spending the night in their house!

The tall Indian walked through the door. Damaris did not know what to expect. She hid in the shadows and stared. Samoset saw her hiding and smiled.

Mrs. Hopkins gave Samoset a rug to sleep on. Samoset wrapped it around his body. Soon, he was sound asleep.

But Damaris did not go to sleep for a long time.

In Part 2 you will learn about more new friends the Hopkinses meet.

AFTER READING

What Did You Learn?

You have read Part 1 of "New Friends in a New Land" for the first time. Now look back at what you wrote on page 44. Did you guess who the new friends would be? What helped you guess? Were you surprised by what you read? What surprised you? Write your answers below.

_____

_____

_____

_____

Check Your Understanding

Darken the circle next to the word or words that best complete each sentence.

1. Damaris Hopkins wished _____ was over.

    Ⓐ fall   Ⓒ spring

    Ⓑ winter   Ⓓ summer

2. Everyone was worried about _____.

    Ⓐ England   Ⓒ Indians

    Ⓑ Damaris   Ⓓ sailing

3. Samoset the Indian learned English from _____.

    Ⓐ Damaris   Ⓒ friends

    Ⓑ explorers   Ⓓ Mr. Hopkins

4. When Samoset saw Damaris hiding, he _____.

    Ⓐ smiled   Ⓒ cried

    Ⓑ sat   Ⓓ hid

Vocabulary — Multiple Meanings

Some words have more than one meaning. The word bow can mean "a weapon." Bow can also mean "tied in a loop." Read this sentence from the story.

> Samoset carried a bow and two arrows.

You can tell that bow means "a weapon." The word arrows is a clue to the meaning. The bow that is used with arrows is a weapon.

Read these sentences about the story. Circle the words that tell the meaning of each word in dark print.

1. The Indians were first to live on the **land** around Plymouth.

   a. to catch   **c.** area

   b. to come down   **d.** go ashore

2. Oceanus started to cry, but the **rest** of the family laughed.

   a. what is left over   **c.** nap

   b. other people   **d.** sleep

3. The sun began to **set** in the sky.

   a. group of things   **c.** ready to go

   b. go down   **d.** put the table in order

4. Samoset was **spending** the night in their house.

   a. buying   **c.** paying money

   b. using up   **d.** passing the time of

Words That Were New to You

Choose words from the story that were new to you. Use a dictionary to check the meanings. Add the words and their meanings to your word list on page 127.

REREADING

Drawing Conclusions

Sometimes writers do not tell everything about a story. Readers use story clues to figure out what the writer means. Read these sentences from the story.

She knew that food was running short. People were dying of sickness. And everyone worried about the Indians.

These clues about the Pilgrims' first winter help you draw a conclusion. The Pilgrims' first winter was very hard.

Reread "New Friends in a New Land," Part 1. Use the story clues below to help you draw a conclusion. Darken the circle next to the conclusion you would draw.

1. Damaris shivered and drew closer to her father. Her father hugged her and her mother gave her a smile. Damaris smiled bravely back.

   Ⓐ Damaris did not want to seem afraid.

   Ⓑ Damaris was not afraid.

2. Samoset had learned some English from explorers. He was eager to talk to the Pilgrims.

   Ⓐ Samoset didn't care about the Pilgrims.

   Ⓑ Samoset wanted to find out more about the Pilgrims.

3. Damaris hid in the shadows and stared. Samoset saw her hiding and smiled.

   Ⓐ Samoset did not like Damaris.

   Ⓑ Samoset thought he would like Damaris.

Word Referents

Pronouns are words that stand for nouns. Read each pair of sentences below. Then, circle the noun or the nouns that the pronoun in dark print stands for.

1. Damaris was glad spring had arrived. **She** ran inside to tell her family.

2. Damaris watched Father and Giles work. **They** were adding thatch to the roof.

STUDY SKILLS

Library Resources

The library has many ways to help you find the information and books you need. You can find out more about the Pilgrims or the Patuxet Indians at the library. Most libraries have both fiction and nonfiction sections.

Fiction books are stories about things that didn't really happen. You can find these made-up stories in the fiction section.

Nonfiction stories are true stories about people and things. You can look for books about the Pilgrims or Patuxet Indians in the nonfiction section.

Reference books are books that you can use only in the library. They are kept in the reference section. Sometimes it is in a special room. This section has encyclopedias.

To find out more about Pilgrims, you could look in the P volume of the encyclopedia. You can also find new magazines and newspapers in the reference section.

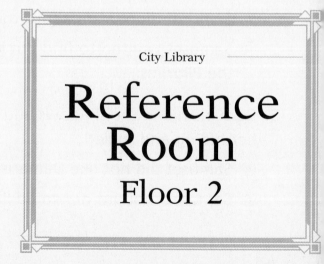

City Library

Reference
Room
Floor 2

Use what you know about the library to answer each question. Circle the correct answer.

1. Where would you find a true book about the Pilgrims?

    nonfiction section   fiction section

2. Where would you find a story in a magazine?

    fiction section   reference section

3. Where would you find a made-up story?

    fiction section   reference section

4. Where would you find facts in an encyclopedia about Samoset?

    nonfiction section   reference section

Check Yourself

Visit your school or neighborhood library. Find two nonfiction books about Pilgrims or Plymouth Colony.

THINK and WRITE

Use what you have learned to complete one of these activities.

1. Imagine that you are Damaris Hopkins. Write a page for your journal about a day in your life. Tell about your trip to America or the new friends you have made.

2. What if you could travel back to 1621? Write what you would tell Damaris. Tell about your family and friends and the games you like to play.

3. Draw a picture for a page of "New Friends in a New Land." Add a sentence to tell about it. Then write why you drew that part of the story.

GETTING READY TO READ

You have read how Damaris met Samoset. In "New Friends in a New Land," Part 2, you will read more about the Pilgrims and the friends they make. You will learn about Thanksgiving in a new land.

What Do You Think You Will Learn?

Look through "New Friends in a New Land," Part 2, on pages 55–58. What do you think you will learn when you read this part of the story? Write your ideas below.

_____

_____

_____

_____

_____

_____

_____

New Friends in a New Land

PART 2

The next day Samoset prepared to leave. He promised to come back to Plymouth again. And he kept his word. A short time later, he came back with a man named Squanto.

Squanto spoke English very well. At one time, he had been kidnapped and taken to England by ship.

Damaris listened to Squanto's story with surprise. The English had done him a great wrong. Yet he still wanted to be their friend.

That same day, a great chief named Massasoit came to Plymouth with sixty Wampanoag Indians. Massasoit's face was painted a dark red. He wore a deerskin over one shoulder and white bones around his neck.

The Pilgrims put out a great welcome. They played the trumpet and drums. They gave Massasoit food and drink. Squanto helped the Pilgrims talk with the Wampanoags. By the end of the day, they signed a treaty. They promised to live as friends in peace.

After that, Damaris stopped being afraid of the Indians. She even became good friends with Squanto. He showed Damaris how to play an Indian game called hubbub. Damaris got so good at it that she could beat Squanto.

Squanto stayed in Plymouth all that spring and summer. He showed the Pilgrims how to dig for clams in the mud by the bay.

He showed them how to plant corn seeds with dead fish to make the plants grow. And he knew which wild berries were good to eat.

Soon, the days grew shorter and colder. Damaris kept busy helping store food for the winter. She picked ears of corn from the fields. She helped salt codfish for winter meals. And she laid out fruit to dry in the late summer sun.

The Pilgrims knew it was time to give thanks to God and their Indian friends. They decided to have a harvest feast. Everyone worked to get ready.

Mr. Hopkins went out hunting. He came back with ducks, geese, and turkey. Mrs. Hopkins baked corn bread and cooked a big pot of fish soup.

Damaris picked herbs from the kitchen garden. She added wood to the cooking fires. And she begged Squanto to bring some Indian children to the feast.

On the big day, Massasoit walked into Plymouth with ninety men. The Pilgrims knew there would never be enough food to go around.

Massasoit fixed the problem by sending his men out hunting. They came back with five deer to roast over the open fire.

Before sitting down to eat, the Pilgrims and the Wampanoags gave thanks. Then they began the feast. Damaris ate until her stomach hurt.

The feast went on and on for three days. Damaris played tug-of-war and pillow pushing with the other Pilgrim children. She watched the Wampanoags dance and sing.

Best of all, she saw a Wampanoag girl who was about her own age. The girl was playing hubbub with her brother. Damaris went up to watch. Soon, she was playing with them.

At sunset on the third day, the Wampanoags went home. Damaris waved good-bye as they walked into the woods. Her new friend turned and waved back.

That night Damaris fell into bed, tired and happy. It had been a wonderful time of thanksgiving.

Like Damaris, we give thanks each year. On Thanksgiving Day, we join our families and friends for prayer, feasting, and fun.

We remember the Pilgrims who started a new life in America. We remember the Indians who helped them. And we remember children like Damaris who worked and played at the first Thanksgiving.

From *New Friends in a New Land: A Thanksgiving Story*, by Judith Bauer Stamper

AFTER READING

What Did You Learn?

You have read Part 2 of "New Friends in a New Land" for the first time. Now look back at what you wrote on page 54. Did anything happen that surprised you? What was the most interesting thing you learned? Write your ideas on the lines.

_____

_____

_____

Check Your Understanding

Read each sentence. Look at the words in the box. Choose one to complete each sentence. Write the correct word on the line.

peace	thanks	treaty	game

1. The Pilgrims and the Indians signed a

   _____.

2. The Pilgrims and the Indians promised to live as friends

   in _____.

3. Squanto showed Damaris how to play an Indian

   _____.

4. Before sitting down to eat, the Pilgrims and the

   Wampanoags gave _____.

Vocabulary — Inflectional Endings

A verb is an action word. When you add -s to a verb, the action happens in the present. When you add -ed to a verb, the action happened in the past. Read these sentences.

1. She begs Squanto to bring children to the feast.

2. She begged Squanto to bring children to the feast.

The word beg is a verb. In sentence 1, -s is added to tell what Damaris does in the present. In sentence 2, -ed is added to tell what Damaris did in the past.

Sometimes, when a verb ends in a consonant, the consonant is doubled before -ed is added. The g is doubled in begged in sentence 2.

Read these sentences. Circle the correct verb to complete each sentence.

1. Damaris meets Squanto. She _____ him and is his friend.

    like   likes   liked

2. Mr. Hopkins walked all over the land. Then he _____ the area.

    map   maps   mapped

3. Damaris was tired and _____ before the feast.

    nap   naps   napped

Words That Were New to You

Choose words from the story that were new to you. Use a dictionary to check the meanings. Add the words and their meanings to your word list on page 127.

REREADING

Summary

A summary is a short retelling of a story. Read this summary of "New Friends in a New Land," Part 1.

> Damaris Hopkins was a young girl who came to America with the Pilgrims. One day an Indian came to Plymouth, where Damaris lived. The Indian told the Pilgrims about their land. The Indian spent the night with the Hopkins family.

The summary is very short. It only gives main ideas and not details. The summary is written in the order in which things happen in the story.

Reread "New Friends in a New Land," Part 2. After you read, think of a short summary for the story. Then complete this summary.

1. Samoset brought Squanto and Massasoit to meet the Pilgrims.

2. The Indians and Pilgrims signed a peace treaty.

3. _____

4. The Pilgrims and the Indians had a Thanksgiving feast that went on for three days.

5. _____

Drawing Conclusions

Sometimes writers don't tell everything about a story. Readers have to use story clues to help them draw a conclusion. Read these sentences. Then draw a line under the conclusion you draw.

> Many Pilgrims died during the first winter. The Pilgrims were running short of food. Squanto taught the Pilgrims how to dig for clams, how to plant corn, and which berries to eat.

1. The Pilgrims liked to eat.

2. Squanto helped save lives by showing the Pilgrims how to get food.

STUDY SKILLS

Encyclopedia

Suppose you want to find out about the people in "New Friends in a New Land." You can look in an encyclopedia. An encyclopedia lists topics in alphabetical order in books, or volumes. Each volume has guide letters.

Here's how to use an encyclopedia.

▶ Look up people by their last names.

▶ Match the first one or two letters of your topic to the guide letters of the volume.

Use the encyclopedia picture to complete the activity. Darken the circle next to the volume number that best completes each sentence.

1. To look up Wampanoags, choose volume _____.

   Ⓐ 21   Ⓒ 3

   Ⓑ 4   Ⓓ 10

2. To look for a drawing of the *Mayflower,* choose volume _____.

   Ⓐ 5   Ⓒ 11

   Ⓑ 13   Ⓓ 7

3. To look up Damaris Hopkins, choose volume _____.

   Ⓐ 5   Ⓒ 9

   Ⓑ 15   Ⓓ 8

Check Yourself

In an encyclopedia look up some people from "New Friends in a New Land." Which ones are real? Which are made up?

THINK and WRITE

Use what you have learned to complete one of these activities.

1. What do you think Massasoit said at the Plymouth Thanksgiving feast? Write a speech for him.

2. Make a model of a tool or toy the Pilgrims or the Wampanoags used in the 1620s. Write about it.

3. Find out what foods the Pilgrims and Indians ate at the Plymouth feast. Make a menu for the feast.

GETTING READY TO READ

The next story you will read is "The Hole in the Dike." A dike is a high wall like a dam that holds back water. This story is about a boy from Holland named Peter. In this story, Peter does something that makes his country very proud. What do you think he will do?

What Do You Think You Will Learn?

Look through pages 65–68 of "The Hole in the Dike," Part 1. Look at the pictures. Think about the name of the story. What do you think this story will be about? Write your ideas below.

_____

_____

_____

_____

_____

The Hole in the Dike Part 1

A long time ago, a boy named Peter lived in Holland. He lived with his mother and father in a cottage next to a tulip field.

Peter loved to look at the old windmills turning slowly.

He loved to look at the sea.

In Holland, the land is very low, and the sea is very high. The land is kept safe and dry by high, strong walls called dikes.

One day Peter went to visit a friend who lived by the seaside.

As he started for home, he saw that the sun was setting and the sky was growing dark. "I must hurry or I shall be late for supper," said Peter.

"Take the short-cut along the top of the dike," his friend said.

They waved good-bye.

Peter wheeled his bike to the road on top of the dike. It had rained for several days, and the water looked higher than usual.

Peter thought, "It's lucky that the dikes are high and strong. Without these dikes, the land would be flooded and everything would be washed away."

Suddenly he heard a soft, gurgling noise. He saw a small stream of water trickling through a hole in the dike below.

Peter got off his bike to see what was wrong.

He couldn't believe his eyes. There in the big strong dike was a leak!

Peter slid down to the bottom of the dike. He put his finger in the hole to keep the water from coming through.

He looked around for help, but he could not see anyone on the road. He shouted. Maybe someone in the nearby field would hear him, he thought.

Only his echo answered. Everyone had gone home.

In Part 2 you will learn how Peter becomes a hero in Holland.

AFTER READING

What Did You Learn?

You have read "The Hole in the Dike," Part 1, for the first time. Now look back at what you wrote on page 64. What did you think this story would be about? Were you surprised? Write your answers below.

_____

_____

_____

Check Your Understanding

Darken the circle next to the word that best completes each sentence.

1. In Holland, the land is kept safe and dry by high, strong
   _____.
   Ⓐ windmills   Ⓒ bikes
   Ⓑ tulips   Ⓓ dikes

2. Peter was riding home when he heard the sound of
   _____.
   Ⓐ geese   Ⓒ rain
   Ⓑ water   Ⓓ wheels

3. Peter put his _____ in the hole in the dike.
   Ⓐ finger   Ⓒ bike
   Ⓑ tulip   Ⓓ eye

4. Peter called for help, but he only heard his own _____
   answer.
   Ⓐ father   Ⓒ echo
   Ⓑ mother   Ⓓ friend

Vocabulary — Contractions

Sometimes two words are put together to make a smaller word. The smaller word is called a contraction.

Two Words	Contraction
do not	don't
I would	I'd
she is	she's

Look at the contractions in the box. The apostrophe like this ' stands for the letters that are left out.

Read these sentences from the story. Underline each contraction. Write the two words the contraction stands for on the lines.

1. Peter thought, "It's lucky that the dikes are high and strong."

_____ _____

2. He couldn't believe his eyes.

_____ _____

Write a sentence of your own with a contraction. Don't forget to use an apostrophe. Underline the contraction you use.

3. _____

_____

Words That Were New to You

Choose words from the story that were new to you. Use a dictionary to check the meanings. Add the words and their meanings to your word list on page 127.

REREADING

Dialogue

In many stories, people in the story talk to each other. When someone is talking in a story, **quotation marks** like this " " go around the words. Look at this sentence from the story.

"I must hurry or I shall be late for supper," said Peter.

The quotation marks tell you what Peter is saying.

Read "The Hole in the Dike," Part 1, again. Look for quotation marks to tell when someone is talking or thinking. Then, look at these sentences. Find them in the story. Write the name of the person who is talking or thinking.

1. "Take the short-cut along the top of the dike."

   (page 66)_____

2. "It's lucky that the dikes are high and strong."

   (page 67)_____

Think of something that someone said to you today. Write one sentence that tells what the person said. Use quotation marks to show the words the person said.

3. _____

   _____

What did you say to someone today? Write one sentence that tells what you said. Use quotation marks to show your words.

4. _____

   _____

Summary

A **summary** is a short retelling of a story. Circle the best summary of "The Hole in the Dike."

1. Peter saw water coming out of the hole in the dike. He tried to stop the water with his finger.

2. Peter had a good time talking to his friend.

STUDY SKILLS

Dictionary — Guide Words

Dictionary words are listed in alphabetical order. Suppose you want to look up tulip. Here's how.

▶ First, look in the T part of the dictionary. Look at the **guide words** at the top of the page.

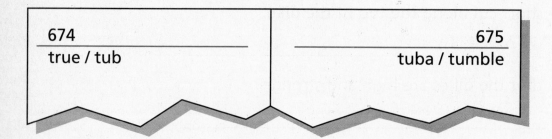

674		675
true / tub		tuba / tumble

▶ Next, look at the second letters in your word and the guide words. U comes after R.

tulip	true / tub	p. 674
	tuba / tumble	p. 675

▶ Then, look at the third letters in your word and the guide words.

tulip	true / tub	p. 674
	tuba / tumble	p. 675

L comes after B in tub. So, tulip is not on page 674.

L comes between B and M. So, tulip is on page 675.

Use the guide words on dictionary pages 674 and 675 to complete this activity.

1. Circle the words that you would find on page 674 between true and tub.

torn	tube	truth
trunk	trap	trouble

2. Circle the words that you would find on page 675 between tuba and tumble.

tugboat	tuck	tryout
trunk	tube	tune

Check Yourself

Find the word tulip in your dictionary. Read the definition. What does it say?

THINK and WRITE

Use what you have learned to complete one of these activities.

1. How would you feel if you were Peter? Would you put your finger in the hole? What else could Peter do? Write about what you would tell Peter.

2. Another name for Holland is the Netherlands. Look up this country in an encyclopedia. Look at the pictures and find a map of the land. Why do you think Holland needs dikes? Use what you find out to write about it.

3. Draw a picture that shows what you know about Holland. Put in tulips, windmills, or dikes. Then, write about the special things in Holland.

GETTING READY TO READ

You have read Part 1 of "The Hole in the Dike." You read how Peter uses his finger to plug a hole in the dike. And you read that no one is around to help him. Can you imagine what Peter is thinking?

What Do You Think You Will Learn?

Look through "The Hole in the Dike," Part 2, on pages 75–78. Do you think Peter will stop the sea from flooding Holland? Write your ideas below.

_____

_____

_____

_____

_____

_____

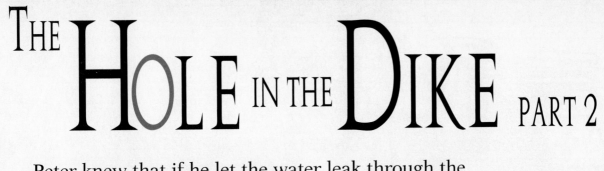

THE HOLE IN THE DIKE PART 2

Peter knew that if he let the water leak through the hole in the dike, the hole would get bigger and bigger. Then the sea would come gushing through. The fields and the houses and the windmills would all be flooded.

Peter looked around for something to plug up the leak so he could go to the village for help.

He put a stone in the hole, then a stick. But the stone and the stick were washed away by the water.

Peter had to stay there alone. He had to use all his strength to keep the water out.

From time to time he called for help. But no one heard him.

All night long Peter kept his finger in the dike.

His fingers grew cold and numb. He wanted to sleep, but he couldn't give up.

At last, early in the morning, Peter heard a welcome sound. Someone was coming! It was the milk cart rumbling down the road.

Peter shouted for help. The milkman was surprised to hear someone near that road so early in the morning. He stopped and looked around.

"Help!!" Peter shouted. "Here I am, at the bottom of the dike. There's a leak in the dike. Help! Help!"

The man saw Peter and hurried down to him. Peter showed him the leak and the little stream of water coming through.

Peter asked the milkman to hurry to the village. "Tell the people. Ask them to send some men to repair the dike right away!"

The milkman went as fast as he could. Peter had to stay with his finger in the dike.

At last the men from the village came. They set to work to repair the leak.

All the people thanked Peter. They carried him on their shoulders, shouting, "Make way for the hero of Holland! The brave boy who saved our land!"

But Peter did not think of himself as a hero. He had done what he thought was right. He was glad that he could do something for the country he loved so much.

From *The Hole in the Dike,* retold by Norma Green

Mary Mapes Dodge told this story to her children more than 100 years ago. She made it up as she went along. But it became so famous that when people visited Holland, they asked about the boy and the dike.

AFTER READING

What Did You Learn?

You have read "The Hole in the Dike," Part 2, for the first time. Now look back at what you wrote on page 74. Did you guess how the story would end? What clues helped you? Were you surprised? Tell why. Write your answers on the lines below.

_____

_____

_____

_____

Check Your Understanding

Read each sentence. Look at the words in the box. Choose one to complete each sentence. Write the word on the correct line.

repair	strength	morning	night

1. Peter kept his finger in the dike all

   _____ long.

2. He had to use all of his _____ to keep the water out.

3. Early in the _____ the milkman saw Peter.

4. The milkman hurried to the village to get men to

   _____ the leak.

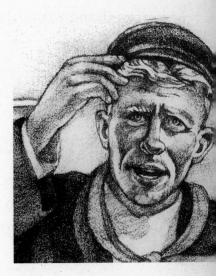

79

Vocabulary — Context Clues

When you see a word that is new to you, you can use other words and sentences to help you find the meaning. Read these sentences.

> Peter knew that if he let the water leak through the hole in the dike, the hole would get bigger and bigger. Then the sea would come gushing through.

Suppose you want to find out the meaning of the word gushing. You know that if the water leaks through, the hole will get bigger. More water will push through the hole. Gushing probably means "rushing out very fast."

Look at each word in dark print. Darken the circle next to the word that gives the best meaning of the word in dark print.

1. Peter looked around for something to **plug** up the hole. He tried a stone and then a stick. They both washed away.

   Ⓐ stop   Ⓒ break

   Ⓑ clean   Ⓓ open

2. Peter asked the milkman to hurry to the village. The milkman told the people there to send men to **repair** the dike.

   Ⓐ town   Ⓒ woods

   Ⓑ field   Ⓓ fix

Words That Were New to You

Choose words from the story that were new to you. Use a dictionary to check their meanings. Add the words and their meanings to your word list on page 127.

REREADING

Sequence

Many stories are told in the order that things happen. One way to keep track of when things happen is to use a chart. Look at this chart.

First	Peter tried to plug the hole with a stone and a stick.
Then	The stone and stick were washed away.
Next	Peter called for help.

Using time order words like first, then, and next can help you keep track. Ask yourself, "What happened first?" "Then what happened?" "What happened next?" Your answers will help you understand the story.

Reread "The Hole in the Dike," Part 2. Then look below at the things that happen in the story. List them in order on the chart.

The milkman brought men from the village.

Peter heard the milk cart.

The men repaired the hole in the dike.

Peter asked the milkman to help.

First	Peter heard the milk cart.
Then	
Next	
Finally	

Dialogue

Complete the sentences. Write the name of the correct speaker or speakers on the line. Use the story to help you.

1. "There's a leak in the dike. Help! Help!"

   _____ shouted. (page 77)

2. "Ask them to send some men to repair the dike right

   away!" said _____. (page 77)

3. "Make way for the hero of Holland!" said

   _____. (page 78)

STUDY SKILLS

Follow Directions

The milkman followed Peter's directions. He went to the village to find people to fix the dike. These tips can help you when you follow directions.

▶ Read all the steps before you start.

▶ Make sure you know what each step means.

▶ Look for words that tell you what to do.

▶ Follow the steps in order.

Read these directions for the milkman to get to the village repair shop.

> Walk straight until you reach the chicken coop. Turn right at the coop. Watch out for broken eggs. Look for a yellow house with a red roof. Turn left. The repair shop is three stores down on the left. Ask for Max.

Use the directions to answer each question.

1. What should the milkman do when he comes to the chicken coop?

_____

2. The milkman sees a yellow house with a red roof. What should he do?

_____

3. After he turns, how many stores down is the repair shop?

_____

4. What should the milkman do at the repair shop?

_____

Check Yourself

Write directions to the lunchroom. Follow them. Were you right?

THINK and WRITE

Use what you have learned to complete one of these activities.

1. Peter deserved a medal for saving the village. Draw a medal you think he got. Tell about the medal.

2. Peter stayed awake all night with his finger in the dike. What would have happened if Peter fell asleep instead? Write how the story might have ended.

3. Be a TV news reporter. Write questions that you would like to ask Peter. Then, write what you think Peter would answer.

3

BE CREATIVE

How are people creative?

Do you ever draw pictures or write poems? That's being creative! No one else can draw pictures or write poems just the way you do. What about your ideas? Maybe you've thought of ways to solve tricky problems. That's being creative, too! There are many ways people are creative. In this unit you will read about how a scientist and a sculptor are creative.

What Do You Already Know?

Think about people you know. How are your friends and family creative? Do they do creative work? Do they solve problems in clever ways? Write about one of these people and how he or she is creative.

_____

_____

_____

_____

_____

_____

_____

What Do You Want to Find Out?

You will find out about two creative people. The famous scientist was a real person who solved some tricky problems. The famous sculptor did something creative for his friends. On the lines below, write some things you want to know about these people. You may find the answers to your questions as you read.

_____

_____

_____

_____

_____

_____

_____

GETTING READY TO READ

The first story you will read is "George Washington Carver, Plant Doctor." Have you heard of this famous scientist? How do you think a scientist could be creative?

What Do You Think You Will Learn?

Look through "George Washington Carver, Plant Doctor," Part 1, on pages 87–90. What do you think you will learn when you read this part of the story? Write your ideas below.

_____

_____

_____

_____

_____

_____

_____

GEORGE WASHINGTON
CARVER,
PLANT DOCTOR
PART 1

Do you like to eat peanuts? Did you know that peanuts are used in many things?

Today, lots of people like to eat peanuts. And lots of things are made with peanuts. But 100 years ago, people did not eat or use many peanuts. Then a man named Dr. George Washington Carver showed people that peanuts are good for many, many things.

Who was George Washington Carver?

George Washington Carver was a scientist who worked with plants. George worked with plants from the time he was a little boy in the 1860s. He gave his plants water, sun, and shade. He raked and weeded.

Farmers would ask George to look at sick plants. George would find ways to make the plants well. George was so good with plants that people called him the "Plant Doctor."

To get to be a real plant doctor, George had to go to school. But that was not easy for George to do. At the time he was a little boy, some schools did not take black students. The school where George lived would not let him in.

So, George had to leave home to go to school. He had to leave Susan and Moses Carver. Susan and Moses were not George's mother and father, but they treated him like a son. George's real mother had been the Carvers' slave. After she died, George lived with them.

George went off to school when he was 12. He missed the Carvers, but he liked going to school. He learned fast. When he learned all he could, he made his way to a new school. To keep on learning, George made his way from school to school for a long, long time.

George made new friends to live with in each new place he went. He helped them with jobs like washing and cleaning. He helped all his new friends grow plants.

Years and years passed. George had learned enough and saved enough to go to college. He was going to be a real plant doctor at last!

George was happy at college. He learned to paint. He learned to sing. And he learned all he could about plants. He did experiments to find out new things about plants.

Soon he was a real plant doctor. He was asked to give classes at the college in Ames, Iowa. Many people came to know of Dr. George Washington Carver and his work with plants.

In Part 2 you will learn about the ways George was creative with peanuts.

AFTER READING

What Did You Learn?

You have read "George Washington Carver, Plant Doctor," Part 1. Think about the things you learned. Then, look back at what you wrote on page 86. What are some ways Carver was creative? Write your ideas below.

_____

_____

_____

Check Your Understanding

Darken the circle next to the word that best completes each sentence.

1. George's real mother was the Carvers' _____.

   Ⓐ sister   Ⓒ slave

   Ⓑ neighbor   Ⓓ doctor

2. From the time he was a little boy, George liked to work with _____.

   Ⓐ doctors   Ⓒ horses

   Ⓑ pets   Ⓓ plants

3. At 12, George left home so he could go to _____.

   Ⓐ school   Ⓒ college

   Ⓑ Iowa   Ⓓ work

4. After many years passed, George became a real plant _____.

   Ⓐ doctor   Ⓒ seller

   Ⓑ farmer   Ⓓ student

Vocabulary — Possessives

To show that something belongs to someone, you can add an apostrophe -s like this 's to the word. Read this sentence.

George's plants grew tall.

You can tell from the 's at the end of George that the plants belong to George. Here's another way to write this sentence.

The plants that belong to George grew tall.

Read the sentences below. Find the word with the 's. Write the word on the line below. Use an apostrophe.

1. George's real mother died.

_____

2. George helped a farmer's sick plants get better.

_____

3. At school, George stayed at a friend's home.

_____

4. George's college years were happy ones.

_____

5. The boy's love of plants helped him learn at college.

_____

Words That Were New to You

Choose words from the story that were new to you. Use a dictionary to check the meanings. Add the words and their meanings to your word list on page 128.

REREADING

Fact or Opinion

Writers tell different kinds of ideas in a story. Some ideas may be facts. Facts are ideas that are true. A writer can prove they are true. Some ideas may be opinions. Opinions tell how a writer feels or thinks about something. Read these sentences.

1. George Washington Carver was a plant doctor. (fact)

2. Plant doctors have interesting jobs. (opinion)

The first sentence is a fact because people can prove that George Washington Carver was a doctor. The second sentence is an opinion. Some people think plant doctors have interesting jobs and some people do not.

Read each sentence. On the line before the sentence, write F if it is a fact. Write O if it is an opinion.

_____ **1.** Carver went away to school when he was 12.

_____ **2.** He must have been very sad when he left the Carvers.

_____ **3.** People did not eat or use many peanuts 100 years ago.

_____ **4.** I think Carver was very happy when he became a doctor.

_____ **5.** Plants are very pretty to look at.

Reread Part 1 of "George Washington Carver, Plant Doctor." Write two more facts from the story.

6. _____

7. _____

Sequence

The order of the things that happen in a story is called sequence. Read each sentence. Then number the sentences 1, 2, or 3 to show the right order.

_____ George became a real plant doctor.

_____ George went off to school when he was 12.

_____ George was happy at college.

STUDY SKILLS

Library

All true stories are called nonfiction. "George Washington Carver, Plant Doctor" is a true story about a real person. This kind of nonfiction story is a biography.

The last story in this unit is "The Last Snow of Winter." It's about something that didn't really happen and people who didn't really live. Made-up stories like this are called fiction.

You can find fiction, biography, and other nonfiction books put in order on the library shelves.

Fiction ▶ Alphabetical order by author's last name. Look for a book by Arnold Lobel under L.

Biography ▶ Alphabetical order by the person's last name. George Washington Carver's biography would be under C.

Other Nonfiction ▶ In order by subject.

M

Where would you find these books in the library? Use what you learned about the library to help you. Circle your answer.

1. fiction book *Journey to Jo'Burg* by Beverly Naidoo

   SHELF: V   Z   N   F

2. book about science experiments with plants

   SECTION: subject   author's last name

3. book about the life of Martin Luther King, Jr.

   SHELF: M   L   K   B

Check Yourself

Go to the library. Find one of the books listed above. Where did you find it?

THINK and WRITE

Use what you have learned to complete one of these activities.

1. How do you think George felt when he went away to school? Write a letter to the Carvers from George. Tell how he would feel and what he would think.

2. The first part of George's story takes place from the 1860s to the 1890s. Find pictures from this time in a book. Write about the people's clothes, houses, and tools.

3. What do you think you will become when you grow up? Write what your biography would tell people.

4. If you could interview George Washington Carver for your school newspaper, what would you ask him? Make up a list of questions.

GETTING READY TO READ

You have read about how hard George Washington Carver worked to become a plant doctor. In Part 2 you will read about the creative ways Carver helped the farmers as a plant doctor. How do you think he helped?

What Do You Think You Will Learn?

Look through "George Washington Carver, Plant Doctor," Part 2, on pages 97–100. What do you think you will learn when you read? Write your ideas below.

_____

_____

_____

_____

GEORGE WASHINGTON
CARVER,
PLANT DOCTOR
PART 2

One man who came to know of George's work was Booker T. Washington. Mr. Washington ran a college for black students. This college was in a place called Tuskegee, Alabama.

Mr. Washington wrote to George. "Our college needs a scientist to help the students learn about plants. You are the best plant doctor we know. Will you come to Tuskegee to help?"

In 1896, George packed his bags. He filled them with seeds and books about plants. He was sad to leave Ames, but he wanted to help at Tuskegee. He wanted to help black students learn.

Tuskegee surprised George. George was used to a college with a fine lab and many books. But Tuskegee was a new college. It did not have lots of things. It did not have a science lab. George had to make a lab with old cups, plates, pots, and pans. He and his students needed a place to work with plants!

George did not work just with students. He worked with farmers, too. At that time, farmers in Alabama needed lots of help. The cotton they planted was not growing well. The farmers had nothing to sell.

George knew why the cotton was not doing well. First, a little bug called the boll weevil liked to eat the cotton plants. And the cotton plants that were left could not get something called nitrogen that they needed to grow well.

All plants need nitrogen to grow well. Plants get nitrogen from the soil they grow in. Some plants take nitrogen from the soil and then put it back. Other plants take nitrogen from the soil but do not put it back.

Cotton plants take nitrogen from the soil but do not put it back. Farmers in the South had been planting cotton for 300 years. Each year, the plants used up more and more nitrogen. Now there was not enough nitrogen left in the soil for new cotton plants to grow well.

George had a way to help the farmers. He wanted them to plant peanuts. Boll weevils do not eat peanuts. And peanuts are plants that put nitrogen back into the soil after using it.

Many farmers did what George said. When they planted peanuts, they had big crops. Boll weevils did not eat the peanuts. And the peanuts put nitrogen back into the soil. Then when the farmers planted cotton another year, the cotton had enough nitrogen to grow well.

Then one day a farmer came to see George. "I planted peanuts," she said. "I want to sell them, but no one wants peanuts! How will I use all of the peanuts? What will I sell?"

At first George did not know what to do. When he had asked farmers to plant peanuts, he did not think about selling them! George knew he had to help!

Then George went to his lab. He did not step outside for weeks and weeks. He mixed and mashed. He did many experiments. He was looking for new ways to use peanuts.

At last George came out of his lab. He had worked for a long time, but he was happy. In the weeks he had worked, he had made lots of things with peanuts.

George used peanuts to make ink, cream, coffee, foods, and many more things. He made more than 300 things, all from peanuts.

Dr. George Washington Carver helped farmers all of his life. He learned many new things about plants that still help people today. He was a plant doctor who helped people, too.

From *George Washington Carver: Plant Doctor*, by Mirna Benitez

AFTER READING

What Did You Learn?

You have read "George Washington Carver, Plant Doctor," Part 2, for the first time. Look back at what you wrote on page 96. What did you learn that surprised you? How was George Washington Carver a creative scientist? Write about it on the lines below.

_____

_____

_____

_____

Check Your Understanding

Darken the circle next to the word or words that best complete each sentence.

1. George Washington Carver taught at a new _____ in Tuskegee, Alabama.

   Ⓐ house   Ⓒ place

   Ⓑ college   Ⓓ room

2. George worked with students and _____.

   Ⓐ children   Ⓒ farmers

   Ⓑ doctors   Ⓓ parents

3. The _____ the farmers planted was not growing well.

   Ⓐ peanuts   Ⓒ corn

   Ⓑ cotton   Ⓓ lettuce

4. All plants need _____ to grow well.

   Ⓐ nitrogen   Ⓒ boll weevils

   Ⓑ experiments   Ⓓ doctors

Vocabulary — Homophones

Some words sound alike but have different spellings and different meanings. These words are called **homophones**. Read these sentences.

1. The Carvers treated George like a son.

2. George gave his plants water, sun, and shade.

Son and sun are homophones. In sentence 1, you can tell that son means "a boy child." In sentence 2, you can tell that sun means "the body in the sky that gives us light and heat."

Read each sentence below. You might need to look up the homophones in dark print in your dictionary first. Then, underline the correct homophone. Circle its meaning.

1. George thought of many **(new   knew)** things to make with peanuts.

   a. was sure about   **b.** not used before

2. The farmers could not **(cell   sell)** their peanuts.

   a. prison room   **b.** get people to buy

3. George had a **(way   weigh)** to help farmers.

   a. put on a scale   **b.** idea

4. George was a plant doctor who helped people **(two   too)**.

   a. also   **b.** a number

Words That Were New to You

Choose words from the story that were new to you. Use a dictionary to check the meanings. Add the words and their meanings to your word list on page 128.

REREADING

Cause and Effect

Sometimes one thing can cause another thing to happen. The thing that makes something happen is the cause. The thing that happens is the effect. Read these sentences from the story.

The cotton they planted was not doing well.

The farmers had nothing to sell.

The cotton they planted was not doing well is the cause. The effect is the farmers had nothing to sell.

Reread "George Washington Carver, Plant Doctor," Part 2. Look for other causes and effects. Ask yourself, "What happened?" and "Why did it happen?" Then, add a cause for each effect in the chart. Look back at the story to help you.

Cause (Why did it happen?)	Effect (What happened?)
	George moved to Tuskegee. (page 97)
	Cotton plants were not growing well. (page 98)
	Farmers had big crops. (page 99)
	George found 300 new ways to use peanuts. (page 100)

Fact and Opinion

An idea that is true is a fact. An idea that tells how someone feels about something is an opinion. Read these sentences. On the line before the sentence, write F if it is a fact. Write O if it is an opinion.

_____ **1.** Cotton plants take nitrogen from the soil but do not put it back.

_____ **2.** I think peanut plants are prettier than cotton plants.

_____ **3.** We know that farmers in the South have been planting cotton for 300 years.

STUDY SKILLS

Encyclopedia — Guide Words

Guide words at the top of each encyclopedia page can help you find what you are looking for. Suppose you are looking for George Washington Carver. Look at the top of these encyclopedia pages.

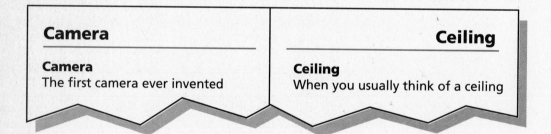

Camera

Camera
The first camera ever invented

Ceiling

Ceiling
When you usually think of a ceiling

Carver   Camera / Ceiling

▶ Car in Carver comes after Cam in Camera.

and

▶ Ca in Carver comes before the Ce in Ceiling.

▶ So, Carver will be on these pages.

Use what you know about guide words. Darken the circle next to the word that best completes each sentence.

1. On the pages with the guide words peanuts and photographs, you can read about _____.

   Ⓐ parrots   Ⓒ penguins

   Ⓑ cotton   Ⓓ whales

2. On the pages with the guide words chickens and clocks, you can read about _____.

   Ⓐ cars   Ⓒ cotton

   Ⓑ China   Ⓓ birds

Check Yourself

Find an article about peanuts in an encyclopedia. What are the guide words at the top of the page?

THINK and WRITE

Use what you have learned to complete one of these activities.

1. Pick a part of George Washington Carver's life that you liked reading about. Write it like a play. Ask friends to help you act it out.

2. Pretend you are giving George Washington Carver an award for creativity. Draw a picture of the award. Write the speech you will give.

3. Become a plant know-it-all. Find out about cotton or peanut plants. Or find out about bugs that harm plants. You can use an encyclopedia or science book. Write what you learn.

GETTING READY TO READ

The next story you will read is "The Last Snow of Winter." Does it snow where you live? How do you feel when it snows? What can you build in the snow?

What Do You Think You Will Learn?

Look through "The Last Snow of Winter," Part 1, on pages 107–110. What do you think you will learn as you read this story? Write your ideas below.

_____

_____

_____

_____

THE LAST SNOW OF WINTER ❄ PART 1

All was quiet in the little French town. The lights in the houses were out for the night. The children were sleeping. The stars were winking.

In a small house an old gentleman was asleep. It was Gaston Pompicard, the sculptor. Once he had sculpted for kings.

He slept soundly. He snored soundly. At his bedside his dog, Louisette, also slept and snored.

When the night was quietest of all, Gaston Pompicard heard a sound. What could it be? A thief?

It was the sound of falling snow.

The first snow of winter, he thought.

He went to the window to see.

The snow fell thickly. It clung to branches and bark, turning the trees to lace. It piled up on doorsteps and bicycles. It whitened the land.

He had a grand idea.

Quickly, he put on his work clothes. Then overcoat, muffler, and beret. All red, his favorite color. He collected his tools. And a blanket.

Gaston Pompicard went to his little kitchen. He heated pea soup for himself and Louisette. It would be cold outside. They should be warm inside.

He opened the door. He and Louisette stood for a moment in the new snow, feeling it fall down upon them.

He ate a snowflake and smiled.

Now he was ready to work.

Stars and street lamps lit the snow.

Gaston Pompicard looked for the right place to work. He saw a patch of snowy ground beneath a chestnut tree. Ah. There.

He flapped the blanket up, then let it settle to the ground. Louisette settled herself upon it.

Then the old man began to work. He piled snow into large mounds. He shaped it. And molded it. He patted and pressed it.

Then he scooped it and chiseled it and gouged it and rasped it with his tools. Last of all he spread snow over everything with a putty knife, as if icing a cake.

Now he was done.

Not quite. Gaston Pompicard went into his house. He brought something back. He put it on his sculpture.

Voilà! He ate a snowflake and smiled. There! "A sculptor for kings is a fine thing to be. But a sculptor for friends is finer."

He and Louisette went back to bed.

In Part 2 you will learn what Gaston has sculpted for his friends.

AFTER READING

What Did You Learn?

You have read "The Last Snow of Winter," Part 1, for the first time. Look back at what you wrote on page 106. Did you learn what you thought you would learn? What were you surprised to learn? Write your answers below.

_____

_____

_____

Check Your Understanding

Choose a word from the box to complete each sentence. Write the word on the line.

snow	slept	clothes
friends	sculptor	

1. Gaston Pompicard was a _____.

2. His dog, Louisette, _____ by his bedside.

3. When Gaston Pompicard looked out the window, he

   saw _____ falling.

4. Gaston put on his work _____ and got his tools.

5. Gaston Pompicard thought that making a sculpture for

   his _____ was a fine thing to do.

Vocabulary — Multiple Meanings

Some words have more than one meaning. The word bark can mean "the sound a dog makes" or "the outside part of a tree." Look at this sentence from the story.

> It clung to branches and bark, turning the trees to lace.

In this sentence, bark means "the outside part of a tree." The words trees and branches are clues.

Read the sentences below. Darken the circle next to the word or words that best tell the meaning of the word in dark print.

1. There was a **patch** of ground that Pompicard liked.

   Ⓐ repair   Ⓒ fix

   Ⓑ piece of cloth   Ⓓ small spot

2. Pompicard looked for just the **right** place to work.

   Ⓐ perfect   Ⓒ not left

   Ⓑ not wrong   Ⓓ close

3. Pompicard patted and **pressed** the large mounds of snow.

   Ⓐ ironed   Ⓒ asked for

   Ⓑ pushed down   Ⓓ picked up

4. Pompicard worked hard, but he did not **tire**.

   Ⓐ get tired   Ⓒ rubber around a wheel

   Ⓑ work faster   Ⓓ cause trouble

Words That Were New to You

Choose words from the story that were new to you. Use a dictionary to check the meanings. Add the words and their meanings to your word list on page 128.

REREADING

Main Idea and Details

A **main idea** is the most important idea in a paragraph. It tells what the paragraph is about. **Details** tell the reader more about the main idea. Read this paragraph from "The Last Snow of Winter."

> The snow fell thickly. It clung to branches and bark, turning the trees to lace. It piled up on doorsteps and bicycles. It whitened the land.

In this paragraph, the first sentence tells the main idea. Other sentences in the paragraph give details about the main idea.

Reread "The Last Snow of Winter," Part 1. Write two details for each main idea below.

1. Main Idea: All was quiet in the little French town. (page 107)

    DETAIL: _____

    DETAIL: _____

2. Main Idea: Gaston Pompicard went to his little kitchen. (page 109)

    DETAIL: _____

    DETAIL: _____

3. Main Idea: Then the old man began to work. (page 110)

    DETAIL: _____

    DETAIL: _____

Cause and Effect

Sometimes one thing makes another thing happen. The **effect** is what happens. The **cause** is why it happens. Use the story to complete the cause and effect chart.

Cause (Why did it happen?)	Effect (What happened?)
Thick snow fell everywhere.	
Gaston wanted to stay warm inside.	

STUDY SKILLS

Story Map

A **story map** can help you remember the important parts of a story. Look at this story map of "George Washington Carver, Plant Doctor."

Story Map	
Setting (where the story takes place)	Alabama
Characters (who the people are)	George Washington Carver Susan and Moses Carver some farmers Booker T. Washington
Main Events (what the important ideas are)	Carver worked with plants when he was a boy. Carver left his family and went to different schools. He had to earn money to go to college.
Ending (how the story ends)	Carver became a plant doctor.

Now use this story map to tell some important parts of "The Last Snow of Winter," Part 1.

Story Map	
Setting (where the story takes place)	_____
Characters (who the people and animals are)	Gaston Pompicard _____ _____
Events (what the important ideas are)	It snows. _____ _____

Check Yourself

Look back at the story to see if your story map is correct. What else could you add?

THINK and WRITE

Use what you have learned to complete one of these activities.

1. What kind of snow sculpture would you make? Draw a picture to show it. Tell about it.

2. Why do you think that Gaston Pompicard thought it was more important to be a sculptor for friends than for kings? Write a paragraph that tells what you think.

3. Suppose your friends made a sculpture of you. Draw a picture of it. Then write about the sculpture.

GETTING READY TO READ

You have read about Gaston Pompicard and how he created a sculpture for his friends. In "The Last Snow of Winter," Part 2, you will read about what Pompicard's friends create for him. What do you think his friends will do?

What Do You Think You Will Learn?

Look through "The Last Snow of Winter," Part 2, on pages 117–120. What do you think you will learn as you read? Write your ideas below.

_____

_____

_____

_____

_____

_____

THE LAST SNOW OF WINTER

PART 2

The sun came out. The children came out. They ran laughing and shouting in the snow.

When they saw the sculpture, they laughed and shouted louder still.

"Look," they cried. "It is us! *Merci,* Monsieur Pompicard! Thank you! *Merci! Merci! Merci!*"

All winter the snow fell. All winter it was beautiful. Gaston Pompicard and Louisette enjoyed it every day. They walked where no one else had walked. They left footprints, both large and small.

Every day they watched the children play.
Sometimes they saw birds fighting for seeds.
Sometimes they watched squirrels seeking nuts. Then
Gaston Pompicard bought hot bread from the baker.
He gave some to the birds. He gave some to the
squirrels. He gave some to Louisette. He gave some to
himself. He ate some snowflakes too.

One day he did not go out in the snow. He stayed
in bed.

He was sick.

He sneezed and sneezed.

"Acheee! Achooo!"

Louisette did not sneeze. But she slept on his bed to keep him company. She stayed there for many days.

Spring flowers were already spiking up. Icicles thawed and dripped. Birds were returning from far away.

Outside, the old man heard the children playing. He felt a little better.

Suddenly everything got *very* quiet. He didn't hear the children. He didn't hear anything except his own sneezes.

When it was quietest of all, he heard a sound. What could it be? A thief?

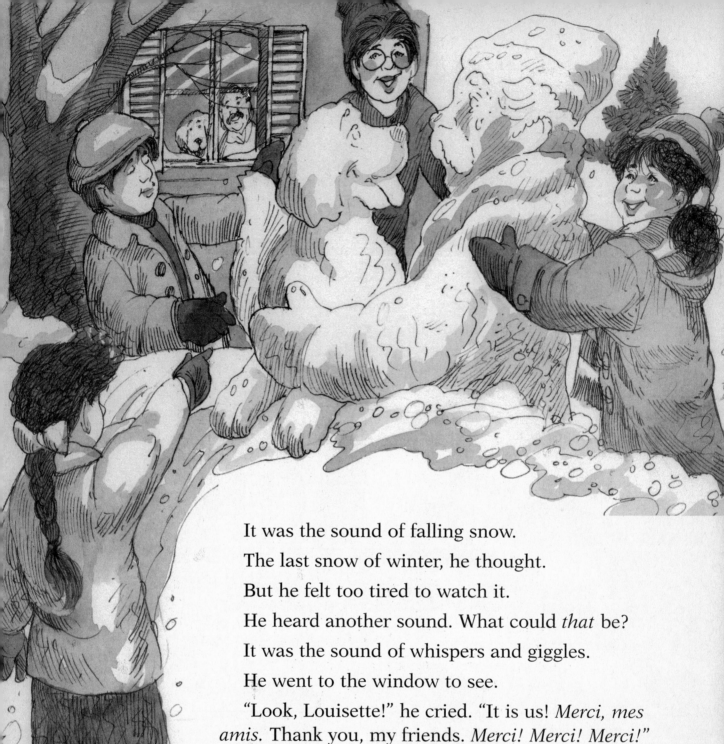

It was the sound of falling snow.

The last snow of winter, he thought.

But he felt too tired to watch it.

He heard another sound. What could *that* be?

It was the sound of whispers and giggles.

He went to the window to see.

"Look, Louisette!" he cried. "It is us! *Merci, mes amis.* Thank you, my friends. *Merci! Merci! Merci!*"

Gaston Pompicard felt much better.

"It is cold outside," he told the children. "Come in, please."

He heated pea soup.

Soon everyone felt warm and happy, eating soup and watching the last snow of winter.

From *The Last Snow of Winter,* by Tony Johnston

AFTER READING

What Did You Learn?

You have read Part 2 of "The Last Snow of Winter" for the first time. Look back at what you wrote on page 116. Were you surprised at what Gaston's friends made for him? Write your answer below.

_____

_____

_____

Check Your Understanding

Darken the circle next to the word or words that best complete each sentence.

1. Gaston Pompicard made a sculpture of the _____.

   Ⓐ winter   Ⓒ children

   Ⓑ dog   Ⓓ house

2. One day Pompicard got _____ and stayed in bed.

   Ⓐ sick   Ⓒ tired

   Ⓑ cold   Ⓓ sad

3. Gaston Pompicard heard sounds and went to the _____ to look.

   Ⓐ door   Ⓒ kitchen

   Ⓑ store   Ⓓ window

4. The children had made _____.

   Ⓐ a mess   Ⓒ a sculpture

   Ⓑ a snowball   Ⓓ footprints

Vocabulary — Compound Words

A **compound word** is made up of two smaller words. Sometimes you can figure out the meaning of a compound word by looking at the two smaller words. Read this sentence.

> Gaston Pompicard and Louisette left footprints in the snow.

Footprints is made up of two smaller words, foot and prints. Think about what each word means. It will help you figure out that footprints are prints made by a foot.

Read each sentence below. Circle the compound word. Then, write the two smaller words on the lines.

1. Gaston Pompicard liked to eat snowflakes.

_____   _____

2. The sculptor liked to wear his red overcoat.

_____   _____

3. Louisette slept by Pompicard's bedside.

_____   _____

4. Gaston was a fine old gentleman.

_____   _____

5. Snow piled up on the trees and doorsteps.

_____   _____

Words That Were New to You

Choose words from the story that were new to you. Use a dictionary to check the meanings. Add the words and their meanings to your word list on page 128.

REREADING

Drawing Conclusions

Sometimes writers do not tell everything about a story. Readers must use story clues to **draw a conclusion**. Read these sentences from the story.

> Louisette did not sneeze. But she slept on his bed to keep him company. She stayed there for many days.

These sentences tell you how Louisette stays near Gaston when he is sick. You can say that Louisette cares about Gaston.

Reread the story. Then, read each sentence below. Darken the circle next to the conclusion you would draw.

1. The children laughed when they saw the sculpture of themselves. They thanked Gaston Pompicard.

   Ⓐ The children didn't like the sculpture.

   Ⓑ The children liked the sculpture very much.

2. Gaston Pompicard took many walks in the snow. He watched the birds and squirrels.

   Ⓐ Gaston Pompicard liked to be outside in the snow.

   Ⓑ Gaston Pompicard did not like the snow.

3. One day Gaston did not go out in the snow. He stayed in bed. He sneezed and sneezed.

   Ⓐ Gaston Pompicard is tired and needs rest.

   Ⓑ Gaston Pompicard has a cold and is sick.

4. He heard another sound. What could that be? It was the sound of whispers and giggles.

   Ⓐ It was the children laughing.

   Ⓑ It was the animals eating.

Compare and Contrast

Complete the compare and contrast chart. Look back at the story to help you.

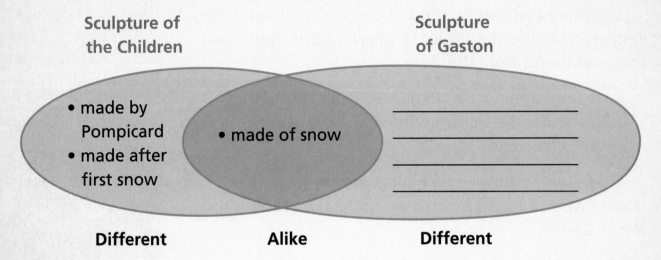

Sculpture of
the Children

Sculpture
of Gaston

- made by
  Pompicard
- made after
  first snow

- made of snow

_____
_____
_____
_____

Different   **Alike**   **Different**

STUDY SKILLS

Table of Contents

A table of contents is found at the beginning of a book. It lists the names of the chapters and the page each chapter starts on. It tells what each chapter is about.

Read this table of contents.

Use the table of contents to answer these questions.

1. What is Chapter 1 about?

   _____

2. Which chapter starts on page 11?

   _____

3. What is Chapter 3 about?

   _____

4. Which chapter tells about a grand idea?

   _____

Check Yourself

Find a book with a table of contents. Turn to the table of contents. How many chapters are in the book? What is Chapter 1 about?

Use what you have learned to complete one of these activities.

1. Imagine that you could create a piece of art for your friends. What would you create? Draw a picture showing what you would make. Then write a few sentences to tell about it.

2. Gaston Pompicard likes to take long walks in the snow. Imagine how he feels as he looks at the birds and squirrels. Write a short poem about what Pompicard thinks as he and Louisette take walks together.

3. What is your favorite season? Why do you like it? Write a paragraph about it.

MY WORD LIST

MY WORD LIST

MY WORD LIST